A Very Happy Christmas

ELISE NOBLE

Published by Undercover Publishing Limited

Copyright © 2016 Elise Noble

v4

ISBN: 978-1-910954-32-4

Edited by Nikki Mentges, NAM Editorial

Cover design by Elise Noble

www.undercover-publishing.com

www.elise-noble.com

For Mason.

Chapter 1

I cycled slowly along the lane, avoiding the frozen puddles that dotted the rutted surface. Frost sparkled on the trees, and through hedges and gateways, I glimpsed the twinkle of Christmas lights, welcoming visitors at this special time of year.

"Not so special for me," I muttered, then chided myself.

Don't be so negative, Marissa.

It might have been the twenty-fifth of December, but for me, it was just another working day. At ten past seven, the same as I always did, I'd left my house to make the mile-and-a-half-long journey to Fairfield House Retirement Home, where I'd worked for the past two and a half years.

As jobs went, it wasn't bad, but sometimes I craved the company of people who were a bit, well...younger. There were only so many games of bingo a girl could take, and don't even get me started on lawn bowls.

Alas, it wasn't to be. According to Barbara's schedule—which she'd decorated with glitter and pinned in the foyer—today, I'd get to enjoy carols at ten, shuffleboard at eleven,

Christmas lunch at twelve, and the Queen's speech at three, followed by a visit from Santa. Fun times.

For a moment, I wished I were back home in Somerset with my family, arguing over which movie to watch and trying to steal cherries out of the Christmas pudding. Right about now, my nephews would be racing downstairs, each trying to get to their stocking first.

I'd been invited, of course, but I'd had to decline. I'd been left with little choice. Had my mother believed my tale about having to feed my next-door neighbours' cat while they took a trip to Casablanca? Probably not, but the deed was done now.

If only I could turn the clock back a few weeks... The problems had all started when I'd accompanied my mother to Mrs. Collins's sip 'n' paint party. With hindsight, *that* was the invite I should have declined. But I'd quite enjoyed art classes at school, and then wine was mentioned... The rest was history.

Mrs. Collins's daughter, Rowena, would be getting married at the end of January, to a lawyer no less, and it was the talk of the village. Everyone from the milkman to old Mrs. Swenson at the post office was speculating about the style of her dress, the colour of her bouquet, and how many bridesmaids would follow her down the aisle. I'd put my money on empire waist, violet, and four—quite literally, because Celia Bainbridge had organised a sweepstake—when the inevitable happened.

"So, Marissa..." Mrs. Collins started. "When are you going to find yourself a nice fellow?"

"I'm not really looking at the moment."

It was true; I wasn't. In fact, I'd been avoiding men since my ex-boyfriend, the man I'd thought was The One, had decided the barista who served up his decaffeinated latte every morning—soy milk, no sugar—gave him a better wake-up than I did.

"Are you sure? Because you're not getting any younger, my dear. Your biological clock is ticking away."

I was only twenty-two, for goodness' sake. I desperately tried to think of a witty reply, but an excess of Chardonnay and a sudden panic that maybe I *would* spend the rest of my life alone meant that when I opened my mouth, nothing came out.

Mum decided to help me, bless her, but several glasses of Pinot Grigio had made her brain-to-mouth filter malfunction, so what actually came out was, "Marissa's not really into men."

Every single mouth fell open, and Celia dropped her paintbrush as well.

Mrs. Willis recovered first, and she patted me on the arm. "Never mind, love. Perhaps you can find yourself a nice lady friend instead?"

No, no, no. I did *not* want to become the subject of village gossip, or worse, matchmaking. The only lesbian in Engleby was Patty Harris, and she had a black belt in judo and scared me a little bit. If I didn't nip this in the bud, we'd be getting joint invitations to supper parties before the week was out.

"What Mum meant to say was that I'm not into *other* men." Good grief, had I lost the freaking plot? "Because I already have one."

My mother turned and stared at me. This was news to her too.

Still, in for a penny, in for a pound. I blathered on regardless. "Yes, I met him at a friend's cheese and wine evening, and he's everything I've always imagined."

Like, totally imagined.

The ladies beamed at me, their pearly whites a sterling advert for denture cleaner. What had I done?

"Congratulations, darling," Mrs. Collins said. "Promise

you'll give me plenty of notice before I need to buy another hat?"

"Absolutely."

Years and years and years.

As I tried to slope off to the bathroom, my mother caught up and grabbed my arm, her excitement bubbling up and spilling over the edges.

"Marissa! Why didn't you tell me?"

"I wanted it to be a surprise," I said miserably.

"Well, it certainly is that. You'll be bringing the lucky chap over for Christmas dinner, then? So we can all meet him?"

What? No!

"I think he's working."

He was definitely working. Christmas Day, Boxing Day, and New Year's too. And because I didn't want to invite an interrogation, I'd had to offer the flimsiest of excuses and dip out on the festivities myself. It was either that or face the entire sip 'n' paint group at church in the morning and have to explain that my beloved had dumped me.

So when Matron asked if I'd mind working on Christmas Day, I decided I might as well. Anything was better than spending the day in my flat—just me, the *Strictly Come Dancing* special, and a turkey dinner for one. Nothing said "loser" quite like a single, pre-packaged turkey breast and an individual bag of microwaveable Brussels sprouts.

No, I'd go to Fairfield House, and if I got really lucky, Mr. Benson might pinch me on the bottom the way he usually did when I got too close.

There was a festive feel to the retirement home when I stepped through the door. We'd spent ages putting up decorations for the residents to enjoy—tinsel and fake snow and mistletoe—and presents spilled out from under the giant Christmas tree in the hallway. It was meant to be a regular-sized tree, but Barbara had read Matron's note upside down, and six feet had turned into nine feet. Mrs. Simpkins's son was a scaffolder, and he'd put it up for us, but goodness only knew how we were meant to get it down again. Ah well, that was a problem for another day. I nudged a gift-wrapped box back into place with my foot. We'd hired an actor to play Father Christmas, and he'd hand the goodies out later.

Since I was a late addition to the rota, I'd been put on entertainment duty for the day—a pleasant change from doing the bed linen and measuring out medication. We started off with karaoke in the lounge, and all the residents joined in enthusiastically, a little too enthusiastically in some cases. I had to put Mr. Benson's teeth back in twice. Bingo went down well too, and by the time the cook served up lunch, everyone was starving.

Yum, dry turkey. I perched on the edge of a chair, pushing food around my plate, half wishing I'd come clean with my family. They'd be exchanging gifts by now. I'd had to post mine and pray Royal Mail delivered them on time.

"Are you staying to watch *Die Hard* with us?" Mrs. Gibson asked.

"Didn't you watch *Die Hard* yesterday?"

"Yes, but it's my favourite Christmas movie."

"Why don't we mix things up and watch *Die Hard 2*?"

"Ooh, lovely."

I happened to know that her daughter had bought her the DVDs of the third, fourth, and fifth movies too. They were sitting under the tree, just waiting to be unwrapped. Well, that was the plan anyway...

Matron waved frantically at me from across the room.

"Santa isn't here," she hissed when I got close enough to hear. "This is a disaster."

"What time did you book him for?"

"A quarter past three, right after the Queen's speech. But he was supposed to arrive at two to get ready."

"It's only five past."

"What if he doesn't show up?"

"Have you called the agency?"

"I don't even have the number. Barbara booked him. She had awful trouble finding someone to work on Christmas Day, but the agency promised he was a professional. Said we'd be in for a real surprise, apparently." Matron folded her arms. "Well, there's nothing for it... You'll have to dress up in the toadstool costume Janice wore for Halloween. It's red and white—with any luck, most of the folks here won't notice the difference."

No. No way. I'd rather have suffered through my mother's pity party than channel an extra from Super Mario.

"I'm not sure—" Oh, thank goodness. Saved by the bell. "That's probably him now."

I practically ran to the front door, hauled it open, and... Wow. Honestly, I had no words. If I'd written a Christmas list, this guy would have been right at the top of it.

"Am I in the right place?" he asked.

"I hope so. I-I mean, I don't know. Are you?"

"I'm looking for Fairfield House."

He even sounded sexy. That low voice was as smooth as a good Merlot. Which I definitely wouldn't be drinking, no siree.

"This is Fairfield House."

He frowned. "But the sign outside said it's a retirement home?"

"Yes, that's right."

Now he looked downright puzzled as he pulled his phone out of a pocket and checked the screen.

"Can I help with anything?" I asked. Literally anything. I'd kiss his freaking feet if he so desired. "Are you lost?"

"This may sound odd, but did anybody here order a stripping Santa?"

Chapter 2

Sexy Santa caught me as I stumbled backwards over the edge of the doormat, and when I failed to regain my balance, he heaved me into a chair in the hallway.

"Are you okay?"

"Oh, fine, fine." Just mortally embarrassed. "Sorry, I went a bit light-headed for a second."

Heat shot up my arm as he took my wrist, checking for a pulse. Was that supposed to help? Because it definitely didn't. His touch turned my insides to liquid.

"I'm still alive," I told him, and he didn't bother to stifle his smile.

"Yes, I can see that. How long since you last ate?"

"About five minutes. I just finished Christmas dinner. Well, I ate the potatoes. The cook does her best, but..."

"Your heart's racing."

"I know that!" I snatched my hand away. "For a moment, I thought you said you were a stripper."

"I did. A lady called Barbara booked me for a show?"

Bloody Nora! This was our jolly old Saint Nick? What had Barbara done, got confused between "Santa" and "Stripper"?

Computers baffled her, and she hated wearing her glasses, so it wasn't beyond the realm of possibility. Until thirty seconds ago, I'd been certain she'd never top the day she mixed up "plumber" and "pall-bearer," but it seemed that maybe she'd managed it. And right now, I wasn't sure whether to freak out or thank my lucky stars.

"Barbara was supposed to book a traditional Father Christmas to give out gifts to the residents. You know—big belly, snowy-white beard, ho-ho-ho."

Santa's dirty cousin started laughing.

"She booked 'the special' and said she wanted the partygoers to have a nice treat."

"What's 'the special'?"

"Everything off."

Oh my... The room went fuzzy, and I started fanning myself.

"If you're feeling faint, it's a good idea to rest for a few minutes. Have you had your blood pressure checked recently?"

"Honestly, I'm fine."

"You should lie down." Santa smiled at me, and his teeth were as perfect as the rest of him. "Trust me, I'm a doctor. Well, almost. I'm a medical student. This gig just pays the bills."

This time when I wobbled, it was because I tripped over a stray walking stick. But that didn't matter to Sexy Santa. He swooped in and caught me before I hit the deck, lifting me effortlessly into his arms. I shrieked as my feet left the floor, then clapped both hands over my mouth because the last thing I wanted was for my colleagues to run in and find me acting oh-so unprofessionally.

"Where to?" he asked. "Is there a couch somewhere? Or a spare bed?"

A bed? Freaking heck, I didn't even dare to think about

what might happen if he put me in a bed. I'd be tempted to drag him into it with me for a preview of his routine. *The special.* Holy hot stuff.

"Uh, the day room on the first floor? It's empty at the moment."

Upstairs, he laid me on the couch and took my hand again. No, not my hand. My wrist again. He was still monitoring my pulse. Santa was doing medical things, and I was imagining him naked because four months of abstinence and two glasses of sherry had made me lose my ever-loving mind.

"Better," he murmured.

Was it? Was it really? I didn't need a health check; I needed a psychiatrist. And anti-klutz pills.

"What's your name?" Santa asked.

"Marissa."

"Marissa. Pretty." He paused, studying me. "I'm Liam. Sit tight, and I'll get you something to drink."

Well, I'd give him eleven out of ten for bedside manner.

I couldn't tear my eyes away from Liam as he walked to the water cooler in the corner and bent to get a paper cup. My heart hammered against my ribcage, threatening to give out in spectacular fashion. Could he hear the *thud-thud-thud*? Part of me wanted to sneak away and expire quietly because hadn't I embarrassed myself already? But the other part was stuck to the spot, staring, because Liam was the kind of magazine-spread-worthy man I daydreamed about, and yet here he was in real-life flesh and blood.

Liam. Leeee-am. I rolled his name around on my tongue. *Nice.* Then I imagined it sliding out of my mouth on a filthy moan.

Oh. My. Goodness. I did *not* just go there.

Liam handed me a cup of water, and I sipped, although it would take a lot more to put out the fire burning in my belly.

Still, it was better than drinking more sherry because that had obviously sent me stupid.

"So...this show. I take it you want me to keep my clothes on?"

Well, no, but...

"You'll stay and give out the presents?"

He shrugged. "A job's a job. At least I'll be able to make someone happy this Christmas."

"I don't suppose that's hard for you," I blurted.

Oh, well done, Marissa. I'd obviously inherited my mum's faulty filter.

For a brief moment, Liam's smile slipped. "You'd be surprised."

I'd take a surprise from him any day.

"Sorry, I didn't mean to..."

"It's okay. Let's just say there's a reason I'm working on Christmas Day."

"Me too," I whispered.

"Bad break-up? Family trouble? Actually, forget it—that's none of my business."

"One led to the other. It all started when my ex got a Starbucks loyalty card."

"Is that better or worse than a new personal trainer?"

For a beat, we simply stared at each other, and then the laughter came. Now I *really* felt light-headed.

"Your ex... A personal trainer?"

"She told me that going to five yoga classes a week was perfectly normal." He made a face. "But enough about me."

"I'd die if I went to five yoga classes a week. Anyhow, uh, thank you for staying."

He glanced at his watch. "I should get changed."

And obviously, his line of work meant he had few inhibitions because he unbuckled his chunky leather belt and dropped his trousers right in front of me.

I screwed my eyes shut and looked away. Cross my heart.

Okay, I didn't.

I totally peeked.

And either he had a couple of hiking socks stuffed down there, or he was very, very good at surprises. Wow. And those abs... I definitely needed to send Barbara a thank-you card—written in large print, of course—and probably a cupcake too.

"Are you feeling better now?" Santa asked a moment later, his voice muffled by a bushy white beard.

Oh, yes. Much better. Even more than much better. My libido would be dining out on this moment for months.

"I'm okay."

Liam held out a hand, and I tried to wipe the sweat off my palm before I took it. He was just being gentlemanly, right? And secretly, I was grateful for his help as he guided me along the corridor and down the stairs. My brain had turned to mush, and there was no telling where my feet would have taken me otherwise. I wasn't even sure which planet I was on.

Yes, I *had* led a sheltered life, thank you for asking.

In the hallway, Liam bent to pick up an armful of presents. Even in a Santa suit, the guy managed to look incendiary. Although I couldn't say I'd be sorry if the fire brigade showed up. Last year, Mrs. Potter had given me a Firemen and Furballs calendar, and phew... I was still stuck on April, and it had nothing to do with the puppy the guy was holding.

"Which way?" Liam asked.

"To the lounge." I pointed at the little arrow on the wall for guidance, mine as well as his.

Liam had the whole package—not only the looks but the sweetness and charm too. Barbara had booked him for an hour, but he stayed for almost three, chatting with the residents and listening to their stories, even Mr. Benson's long-winded tale about the Second World War. And when the

11

finale of everyone's favourite dancing show came on, he squashed onto a sofa between me and Mrs. Simpkins and watched the whole thing.

My thigh was wedged against his, our sides touching, and I had to remind myself to breathe deeply so I didn't hyperventilate. Although inhaling Liam's cloud of pheromones probably wasn't helping matters. He shifted in his seat, and sheesh, the man had muscles. I upgraded Barbara from a thank-you card and a cupcake to a whole bakery because Liam's smiles were the nicest Christmas gift I'd ever received.

But all too soon, the joy was over.

It wasn't every day a man gave me a second glance, not one my age anyway, and I felt strangely sad as I led him towards the front door. Ah, well. Every fairy tale had to end, and mine was no exception.

At least this year, I'd had a very happy Christmas after all.

Chapter 3

"Thanks for the hospitality. And the food."

"Hey, you earned it."

Liam was back in his street clothes now, and he raked a hand through already-tousled hair.

"After the mix-up, this could have been awkward," he said.

"You were great with the residents. And I'm sorry Mrs. Potter kept pinching your bottom."

"It's not the first time that's happened, and it won't be the last. Who was the lady that kept humming the theme song from *The Full Monty*?"

"Miss Hartley."

"She was fun. And this might not be entirely appropriate, but you should get the mole on her neck checked out. It looks atypical to me, and it could be precancerous."

"Really? I'll definitely pass the info along to Matron."

Liam leaned closer to tuck a stray lock of hair behind my ear, and a shiver ran through me, quickly followed by the horrible realisation that I'd never see him again. When he leaned in and kissed me on the cheek, heat burned in my veins.

"Nice meeting you, Marissa."

"Aren't you going to say goodbye?" Mrs. Potter poked her head through the doorway to the lounge. "Marissa, you can't keep Sexy Santa all to yourself, you young hussy."

I gave Liam an apologetic grimace. "Would you mind?"

"Sure."

"And I'm not a hussy, I swear. In fact, I've only had one serious boyfriend, and— Uh, you definitely don't need to hear the details."

Liam just laughed as he strode back to the lounge. The goodbyes took a full ten minutes, but he didn't complain, not once. However much Barbara had paid him, it wasn't enough.

Then he turned to leave, for real this time. As he walked past me, he paused for a beat, then lowered his voice so only I could hear.

"I don't normally do private shows, but for you, I'd make an exception." He stepped back and raised an eyebrow, questioning. "No strings."

Holy moly, did that mean what I thought it did? A vision of his naked backside flashed into my head, and I had to clench my jaw to stop my tongue from hanging out. Was he serious? He looked serious, standing there with a delicious little smile tugging at the corners of his lips.

I swallowed hard and then nodded. Perhaps Mrs. Potter knew me better than I knew myself.

"I'll wait outside. Black BMW," Liam whispered, and then he was gone.

Oh, yes. This was going to be a very, *very* happy Christmas.

Chapter 4

A *year later...*

I cycled slowly along, trying to avoid the mud. The council had resurfaced the lane not so long ago, which meant the potholes that had been the bane of my life for so many months were gone, but after the road opened to traffic again, the local farmer had celebrated the improvements by driving his tractor here, there, and everywhere. The slippery mess he'd left behind was worse than the potholes, and the odour of rotting Brussels sprouts filled the air.

The fourth house on the left had been sold in the summer, and its new occupants seemed determined to outdo all the neighbours in terms of electricity consumption. They'd decorated every inch of brickwork with lights and even had a replica stable on the front lawn, complete with a wailing baby Jesus.

I shuddered and carried on pedalling.

Sure, it was Christmas Day, but I couldn't help wishing it were over. Oh, I used to enjoy the festive season, but now every time I saw a Santa decoration, my insides clenched and I felt a little bit queasy. Funny how one bad experience could taint the rest of your life, wasn't it?

At ten past seven, just as I always did, I'd left my house to make the mile-and-a-half-long journey to Fairfield House Retirement Home, where I'd worked for the past three and a half years. As jobs went, it wasn't bad, but the residents weren't getting any younger and a part of me still longed to spend time with people I had more in common with. Yet every time I thought of moving on, a fear of the unknown held me back. My one attempt at being impulsive last year had resulted in disaster. Best not to try again, eh?

Instead, I was due to enjoy a festive play written by Mrs. Simpkins at ten, non-alcoholic mulled wine at eleven, Christmas lunch at twelve, a visit from Santa at two, and the Queen's speech at three, according to Barbara's laminated timetable. She'd decorated it with spray snow and pinned it up in the foyer.

Things could have been worse, but a part of me still longed for the old family Christmases I used to love back home in Somerset, arguing over who the final cracker belonged to and trying to steal the last drop of port. Right about now, my nephews would be stealing each other's Lego and making themselves sick as they gorged on selection boxes before breakfast.

But going home for Christmas was out of the question. Firstly, because our traditional get-together had been postponed, and secondly, because I'd done something incredibly foolish.

My bike's front wheel wobbled as I recalled the conversation I'd had with my mum a fortnight ago in horrifying detail.

"I've got wonderful news," she'd announced the instant I picked the phone up.

"What's that?"

Had my sister won another hairdressing award? Did her husband get that promotion he'd been after?

"We're moving Christmas."

"Sorry?"

"We missed you last year, and since you have to work on Christmas Day, we thought we'd celebrate on New Year's Day instead. Plus your dad and I got a great deal on a cruise around the Balearics during Christmas week. I've always wanted to go on a cruise."

"Uh…"

"You don't have to work, do you? Last year, you said that if you worked over Christmas, you got New Year's off."

"That's right, but—"

"So we'll see you on the first of January, then? With that boyfriend of yours? We're all dying to meet him."

Yes, my boyfriend.

My *imaginary* boyfriend.

Now do you see why I could never attend a family dinner again?

"Uh, we can't make it." *Think, Marissa. Think.* "Liam's sister's getting married, and we promised to go to the rehearsal."

"A wedding rehearsal? On New Year's Day?"

"I know, it sounds a bit odd, doesn't it?"

Dammit, I needed to start thinking of these excuses in advance so I'd have a repertoire of good ones. Mum hadn't sounded convinced by my need to attend Liam's second cousin's christening in the summer, or by us visiting his uncle for Easter lunch either.

"I'm surprised the vicar agreed to work on that day."

"Apparently, he needs the extra money for the church

roof." *Ouch.* Even I winced at that one. "There's a leak. Right above the altar."

"Oh, Marissa, we haven't seen you for ages. You need to come and visit."

"Soon, Mum. I promise. I'll come home soon."

When I hung up, I'd spent a full minute with my head in my hands. One little lie about dating a man totally out of my league had spiralled beyond all control.

The initial mistake had been compounded by last January when Patty Harris's younger brother had asked me out for dinner in front of the entire Rotary club. Flattering, but oh-so awkward. I liked him, I did, but not in *that* way, and since everybody was staring at us, I'd done my best to let him down gently.

Before I knew it, I'd told the crowd watching us about my lovely boyfriend, Liam. A newly qualified doctor, no less. Mum kept dabbing at her eyes with a tissue, and she'd looked so overjoyed at the idea of me dating again that I couldn't bring myself to tell her the truth. Now embarrassment kept the stories spilling from my mouth, a river of lies for me to drown in.

Liam.

The boyfriend I absolutely did not have. In fact, the mere mention of the man's name made me break out in a cold sweat. And after what had happened on Boxing Day last year, who could blame me?

Because Sexy Santa was a lying swine.

I blocked all memories of Liam from my psyche as I parked my bicycle under the smoking shelter at the side of Fairfield

House. This year's celebration would be a stripper-free zone. No dimpled smile. No heart-melting grin. No butt cheeks so taut I kept running my fingers over them to check they were real.

Just to make sure, I'd personally booked the Santa to deliver the residents' presents this year, and the lady at the agency had promised to send the ugliest old man on the books.

Boy, did she deliver.

The doorbell rang at two thirty, and I hurried to let in our bringer of Christmas cheer.

"Have you got any sherry?" he asked before he'd even got both feet over the threshold.

"Pardon?"

"Sherry. Have you got any sherry?"

"Uh, I think we might have a drop in the kitchen."

"And a couple of mince pies, love." He patted me on the bottom as I led the way inside. Was he secretly related to Mr. Benson? "Where do I change?"

"We've got a spare room set up for you."

Mrs. Jones had died last week, so I'd packed her belongings into cardboard boxes and stacked them in the wardrobe until her daughter could pick them up. The death of a resident was never a good thing, but we'd have been short of space otherwise.

"Good, good. The sooner this is over with, the sooner I can get back to *Only Fools and Horses.*"

At least he's not Liam. At least he's not Liam, I chanted in my head as he followed me up the stairs. His beady eyes burned into my behind like red-hot coals. Pervert.

"Here you go. There's a mirror in the bathroom if you need it."

"Before you disappear, I'm going to need a hand with the buttons, love."

A little bit of bile rose into my throat.
At least he's not Liam.

Chapter 5

"I didn't like that Santa," Mrs. Simpkins told me after the grubby git had belched his way through the present-giving. "What happened to the nice young man who came last year?"

"He wasn't available."

"Shame. If I'd been fifty years younger, I'd have offered him an extra Christmas gift of my own. I bet that chap knows how to show a girl a good time."

Oh, he did.

He most definitely did.

He also knew how to break a girl's heart and leave her wallowing in wine and ice cream for weeks afterwards. Maybe even months.

Liam.

The man who'd given me the best night of my life, and then ruined it.

The man who'd taken up far too much of my headspace in the weeks that followed.

The man who'd proven impossible to forget, no matter how much I wanted to.

And it was his name I'd blurted out to Richie Harris because I was an idiot. Dammit.

This time last year, when Liam had propositioned me in the hallway after *Strictly Come Dancing*, I'd been happier than a supermodel at a salad bar. I couldn't wipe the big stupid grin off my face when I dashed out after my shift and slipped into his BMW around the corner. Me! With Liam's looks and charm, he could have had any girl he wanted, and he'd picked *me*.

He flashed a quick grin as I closed the passenger door. "I wasn't sure you'd come."

"Neither was I," I admitted. "I've never done anything like this before."

"It's a first for me too." He reached for my hand, and I almost had a coronary when he brought it to his lips and kissed it. At least he could have resuscitated me afterwards. "But I couldn't walk away from your smile, not without trying my luck. There's something special about you, Marissa."

The way he said that, I'd almost believed it. But it was just a damn line. I realised that now.

"So, what do we do next?"

"I don't know. I didn't exactly plan this." For the first time, he looked uncertain. "You want to come to my place? I'd take you out for dinner, but I doubt anywhere's open today."

He was basically inviting me over for sex, wasn't he? I'd never thought of myself as the type of girl to have a one-night stand, but then again, I'd never imagined myself climbing into a virtual stranger's car either. What if he was an axe murderer?

I met his gaze, and those bottomless blue eyes did funny things to my insides.

"Your place sounds good."

At least I'd die happy.

And to be fair, Liam *did* make me happy. Ecstatic, even. Until I woke in the morning and found he'd disappeared. His flat wasn't all that big—only one bedroom—and he definitely wasn't in it. Growing twitchier by the second, I'd wrapped the bed sheet around me and checked every room. Kitchen, bathroom, living room, even the tiny hallway. And a couple of the cupboards. Okay, so he'd have had to be a contortionist to fit in those, but I was freaking out by that point. If he'd gone to work, wouldn't he have left a note? Or kissed me goodbye? I found last night's Santa suit as well as a cowboy outfit and a policeman's uniform, but no Liam. The air was still. Quiet. Empty.

Then the phone on the hall table rang, and I jumped out of my skin. *Relax, Marissa. Having a phone is perfectly normal.* Wasn't it? Didn't most people have mobiles nowadays? Perhaps Liam was an old-fashioned kind of guy, which wasn't necessarily a bad thing because people spent far too long staring at tiny screens, but... Oh, there was an answering machine.

"This is Liam, you know what to do."

"Hello? Liam? Daaaaarling? I'll be around in half an hour with a special surprise for you." The woman's voice dropped low and smoky. "And then I need you in my bedroom."

What the hell...? My guts seized and bile rose in my throat. Who was this woman? What surprise? And why did she need him in her bedroom? Surely there was only one reason with a man like Liam?

Granted, we hadn't discussed our relationship statuses before we...you know, but I'd assumed he was single, the same as me. Clearly, I'd been mistaken. That rat!

Okay, damage control was required. Another woman was on her way over, and I didn't want to be naked when she arrived. I hastily pulled my wrinkled dress over my head and finished doing up the buttons. Where were my knickers? I found my bra hanging over the wardrobe door, but where were my freaking knickers?

And where was Liam?

He still hadn't come back by the time I tied my shoes, and I almost tripped over running out of the bedroom. *Hurry, hurry, hurry...* If the woman matched her voice, a vixen was about to turn up, and I didn't know how to deal with her. I took a last look around, and that was when I noticed them.

No, not my knickers. I'd given up on those. The pictures. A shelf full of them in the living room—Liam with his arm around a gorgeous brunette. Was she the owner of the voice on the phone? She had the polished, sophisticated look that I could never hope to achieve as she stood at his side in a cocktail dress, in a smart suit, in a bloody bikini. Heck, I didn't even own a cocktail dress, or a bikini, and I only wore a one-piece when I had a kaftan to cover it up with.

And I'd never have a man like Liam. Not really, not for more than one night. A night when he'd obviously been feeling horny and resorted to the first piece of warm flesh to satisfy himself.

Dammit. I snatched a tissue from the box on the sideboard and wiped my eyes. How could I have fallen for his lines?

Never again would I be so stupid. *Never again.*

Back in the real world, a sickening *thump* followed by a loud groan broke me out of my thoughts, and I ran through to the hallway to see what had happened. Matron had got there before me, and she was comforting Mr. Benson on the floor where he'd landed.

"Missed the last step," he muttered, grimacing as he shifted to one side. "Owwww. It's my hip."

"Call an ambulance," Matron instructed.

I already had my phone in my hand, and half an hour later, we watched as a pair of paramedics loaded Mr. Benson into the back of an ambulance.

"Can you go to the hospital with him, Marissa? I'll sign off on the overtime."

"Of course." Mr. Benson was a sweet old man, even if he did insist on pinching my bottom every time I walked past, and I had a nasty suspicion he might have broken a bone in that fall. "Could you give Mrs. Simpkins her pills? I haven't done that yet."

Matron squeezed my hand. "I will. Thank you, sweetheart."

My last visit to the hospital had been almost a year ago when I took Miss Hartley to get her mole removed. I couldn't say I felt overjoyed at the thought of spending the rest of Christmas Day there, but at least I wouldn't be moping at home. I only hoped they had a decent selection of magazines in the waiting room.

With the lights and sirens on, the trip went quickly, and Mr. Benson was soon being wheeled into A&E, a little woozy from the pain medication they'd pumped into him but otherwise in good spirits. I trailed in behind, feeling like a spare part in the whirl of efficiency.

"What seems to be the problem here?" the doctor asked.

"Suspected hip fracture," the paramedic replied, handing over the paperwork.

No, no, no. I closed my eyes, hoping that when I opened them, this would all turn out to be a bad dream. Surely a girl couldn't be this unlucky?

Oh, who was I kidding?

Of course I could.

Ever since I'd first laid eyes on Liam, my life had been plagued by mistakes, and today was no different. Because there he was again, wearing a pair of scrubs and peering at Mr. Benson's notes, large as life and twice as handsome.

Please, somebody kill me now.

Chapter 6

Maybe if I turned and ran, Liam wouldn't see me?

I glanced down, thankful I had my sensible shoes on. Plain grey Mary Janes with memory-foam insoles. *You can do this.* Slowly, carefully, I backed away, aiming for the exit. Mr. Benson would be okay on his own for a few minutes—the happy pills had kicked in, and he was flirting with one of the nurses now. If I called Matron and explained the situation—obviously not the part about my sexcapade but that I felt quite, quite sick—she'd send someone else to cover.

Yes. That was a good plan. My phone was in my pocket, and I always kept a ten-pound note in its case for emergencies. That would pay for my bus fare home. My neighbour had a spare key, and I could go back to Fairfield House for my handbag tomorrow.

"Marissa?"

Oh, hell.

Dread pooled in my belly as I looked up to find Liam staring right at me.

What were the chances of him believing I was somebody else? Everyone had a doppelgänger somewhere, right?

Liam studied the chart in his hand. "You're still working at Fairfield House?"

I bit my lip to hold in my groan. "Yes, I am."

"Oh." There was that uncertainty again, the slight pursing of his lips that I'd first seen in his car a year ago. "I wasn't sure. I mean, when I called..." He gave his head a shake. "You look...well."

"Uh, you too. I see you got a new job."

For a second, the cocky smile I remembered flashed across his face, and then it was gone. "Yeah. Finally graduated."

"Congratulations, Dr. Liam."

"Dr. Carlisle, actually."

Liam Carlisle. That went nicely together. Did he have a middle name? *Carlisle.* Liam and Marissa Carlisle. *Dammit, Marissa!* Stop. Liam might have been extraordinarily hot, but I'd already been burned once. No way was I about to stick my fingers in the fire again. Or my tongue. Or any other part of me.

Fortunately, Mr. Benson saved the day. "Got any more of those painkillers, boy?"

"Let's get you through to an exam room, Mr. Benson."

Liam flashed me one more tight smile, then walked out of my life for the second time.

Gee, that wasn't awkward at all.

Hospital coffee tasted disgusting. Burnt and gritty, as if someone had emptied the contents of a dustpan into the cup and given it a good stir. Or perhaps it was just me that was bitter?

Liam had obviously moved on after doing the nasty with

me last year. I mean, look at him now—scrubs, stethoscope, fancy title. And there was me, still stuck in the same dead-end job with my imaginary boyfriend and a lousy chocolate habit.

Last Christmas, for a few hours, he'd given me hope I could make more of myself, that there was something more to life than work and Netflix binges, but I should have known better. Girls like me didn't date men like Liam, not outside of romcoms, anyway.

But for one day, just one day, I'd dared to think differently...

When I agreed to go home with him, I hadn't been sure what to expect. Was conversation required during a one-night stand? Or did people simply shed their clothes, do the deed, and then mutter a hasty "thanks" before they parted ways?

"Want to take a seat?" he'd asked as he closed the front door behind us.

"A seat?"

He waved at the sofa visible through an open door. "Do you want tea? Coffee?"

"I wouldn't mind a coffee."

Not because I was thirsty but because it would give me a moment to get my thoughts in order.

"Something to eat as well?"

"We had a turkey lunch at Fairfield House before you arrived."

"That was hours ago."

Yes, but I'd lost my appetite for everything but Liam. He was a salted-caramel muffin of a man—delicious, moreish, but no good for me in the long run.

"I'm not really hungry."

He made us proper coffee in a French press, not instant, and took a seat next to me. My thoughts were still a jumbled mess. Had I lost my mind? Probably, but at that moment, I didn't particularly care to look for it. Outside, the sky was dark save for a sliver of crescent moon, and he'd dimmed the lights in the living room, so I probably wouldn't find much anyway.

"You're nervous, aren't you?"

"How did you know?"

He uncurled my left hand from its death grip on the hem of my dress and held it in his, stroking my knuckles with his thumb.

"Because you haven't smiled once since you got here."

"Sorry."

"There's nothing to be sorry for. It's me who should apologise for coming on strong earlier. It's just... I don't know. You were so damn tempting."

I forced myself to unclench my other hand. "Tempting?"

"I knew if I walked away, I'd kick myself later."

He ran his other thumb over my bottom lip, barely a graze, but my skin burned from his touch as my heart hammered against my ribcage.

"Do you know CPR?" I blurted.

"It was pretty much the first thing they taught us at medical school."

"Sorry, that was a dumb thing to ask, but I... I..."

"Relax." Liam settled back against the cushions and casually draped an arm across the back of the sofa. "Let's just enjoy each other's company, okay? Want to watch a movie?"

"A movie?"

"James Bond's on. If you don't want to take things any further, I'm not going to push my luck."

But I *did* want to take things further. As James Bond blew up cars and got his girl, I snuggled back against Liam and he curled an arm around my shoulders. What would *he* look like in a tuxedo? Or better yet, out of one? Sexier than 007 if the glimpses I'd snuck earlier were anything to go by. I fidgeted as he focused on the TV screen, way, way out of my depth. What was I even doing here?

As the closing credits rolled, Liam tilted my chin towards him. "So... You want to watch another film?"

I shook my head, and he raised an eyebrow, expectant.

Hmm, how did I put this into words? My experience with men was limited to a single ex-boyfriend, one who made lawn bowls look exciting. A romantic evening with him had consisted of a bit of perfunctory kissing followed by a quickie in the missionary position, and if I was lucky, he'd made me a cup of tea afterwards. But Liam... Liam was skydiving, the entire Kama Sutra, and one of those fancy cocktails with the little umbrellas on the side.

And the longer I stared at him, the darker his gaze became. Now he was looking at me the way a lion watches its prey.

"You want me to kiss you?" he asked.

Oh, thank goodness.

I nodded, beyond relieved that he was taking the lead.

His lips brushed across mine, and then he waited for a beat. I nodded again, letting him know I was okay, and this time, the kiss was deeper with a hint of tongue. He still tasted of coffee, rich and strong, and I inhaled his musky scent as he pulled me against him. Hard. I forgot about my lack of experience as instinct took over. Stubble scratched at my palms as I cupped his cheeks, and his hands roamed over my exposed skin, burning me with every caress.

Who was this lunatic and what had she done with Marissa? I scrambled into his lap and ground against his hardening cock, and when I closed my eyes, all I could see was his naked ass. I'd only caught a glimpse earlier, but it was still a memory to treasure. Before I could stop myself, I'd reached under his shirt and run my hands across his smooth chest.

As my hand paused over his heart, he trapped it under his own. "You want to move this to the bedroom?"

"I think so."

"You think? You need to be sure."

I swallowed hard. "I'm sure."

The things he did to me that night still made me blush when I thought about them, still made my thighs clench, and he'd ruined me in more ways than one.

He'd broken my heart.

Silly, I know, considering I'd only just met him, but in a few short hours he'd worked his way inside both physically and metaphorically. And even though he'd hurt me in the end, I knew, I absolutely knew, that I'd never find another man who measured up to his, ahem, talents.

Chapter 7

I was staring into a flimsy plastic coffee cup in the hospital waiting room, contemplating the many, many mistakes I'd made in my life, when a shadow slid into the seat beside me.

"Mr. Benson's got a broken hip."

Oh, great. Liam was back. I focused on the floor, willing myself to breathe slowly and hoping my face wasn't too flushed from the memories of *that* night.

"What'll happen to him now?"

"We've taken X-rays, and he's scheduled to have the bones pinned tomorrow. Do you know how to get hold of his family? He was too busy propositioning the nurse to tell me. I think the paramedics might have got slightly carried away with the morphine."

Deep breaths, Marissa. At least Liam was keeping this professional.

"His family lives in Australia. Near Sydney, I think? Matron has the contact details, but his daughter's only been to see him once in the last four years, so I doubt she'll come rushing over here."

"I see too many patients with kids like that."

The sadness in his voice made me look up, and I took the chance to study him more closely. Last year he'd been full of energy, but today, black circles darkened the skin under eyes that had lost their sparkle. Maybe working as a doctor wasn't all it was cracked up to be?

A bit like life, really.

"It's the same at Fairfield House. Half of our residents have been abandoned." I couldn't resist getting a little dig in. "I know the feeling."

"Marissa..."

I rose to my feet. "Well, I'd better head off. Thanks for looking after Mr. Benson."

"Marissa, please..."

The doors behind us flew open and a young woman rushed in, clutching a limp child in her arms.

"Somebody help! He's stopped breathing. His face swelled up, and he stopped breathing. Please, help him!"

Liam leapt up and called for a nurse. "What happened?"

"He was eating sweets, and then he couldn't breathe."

"Does he have any allergies?"

"No. I mean, I don't think so? He's my sister's son, and she flew out to Spain yesterday and left him with me."

"What's his name?"

"Pharaoh. Pharaoh Baxter."

Pharaoh? Ouch.

"Can you call your sister?"

"I can try."

Liam disappeared with a gaggle of nurses and the young patient, leaving the girl alone in the waiting room. Tears dripped down her cheeks and splashed onto the tiled floor, so I rummaged around in my pocket until I found a crumpled packet of tissues. Carrying them had become second nature, what with all the spillages at Fairfield House.

"Here, use these."

She took them with a trembling hand and wiped her eyes. "What should I do? I hardly know anything about children, but if I hadn't offered to look after him, my sister would have left him in her hotel room while she went out clubbing."

Boy, her sister sounded like a delight.

"The doctors'll take good care of your nephew. They're really professional here."

"But what if...what if...?"

I led her over to the seats Liam and I had just vacated. "Why don't you sit down, and I'll find you a cup of tea? Then we can make that phone call. I'm Marissa, by the way."

She managed a watery smile. "Charlene."

Hours passed while Charlene gripped my hand, and I heard all about her nightmare of a sister and how it wasn't the first time she'd abandoned the son she'd never wanted in the first place. Two months ago, the woman had headed off to Scotland, and the month before that, to Blackpool, each time with a different guy. Charlene did her best with her nephew, but at seventeen, she wasn't much more than a child herself. Her sister hadn't even answered the phone on the five occasions we'd tried to reach her.

Hearing the details of Charlene's situation made me all the more grateful for my own family, and I cursed myself for the problems I'd created with my Liam-lies over the past year. I needed to come clean and admit what I'd done, sooner rather than later. Yes, I'd be mortally embarrassed, but that was better than being alone.

Charlene was halfway through her third cup of tea when Liam reappeared, and he looked terrible. Exhausted, as if he could barely hold himself up.

"Your nephew's going to be okay. He went into anaphylactic shock, but he's stable now."

Charlene threw her arms around him, and he stumbled back a couple of steps.

"Thank you! Thank you so much."

"We'll need to keep Pharaoh in for tests, but it looks as if he has a peanut allergy."

"A peanut allergy? But...but I'm sure he's eaten nuts before, and he was fine."

"Allergies can develop at any age. What's important is that you learn how to manage it. He'll need to keep an EpiPen with him at all times from now on, and you and your sister will have to monitor everything he eats very carefully."

Charlene chewed her lip, and I knew what she was thinking—if her sister stayed true to form, she'd probably give Pharaoh a Snickers bar for breakfast.

"Can I see him?" she asked Liam. "Please?"

"A nurse will take you through."

Charlene turned and gave me a quick hug. "Thanks so much for staying. I don't know what I'd have done on my own."

"I hope everything goes well. And I know it's hard, but you need to speak to your sister. She can't keep doing this to you."

"I will," Charlene promised, but I knew she wouldn't. She was like me—flight rather than fight, every time.

As she trailed the nurse through the double doors, Liam sank back in the chair next to me, closed his eyes, and sighed.

"You did good," I told him. "You saved that boy's life."

"That story's nothing new, unfortunately. Next week, there'll be another Pharaoh Baxter, and he might not be so lucky."

"No, he might not have a caring aunt who brings him to the hospital and also stops his mum from naming him Typhus."

Liam chuckled, then realised I wasn't laughing. "Wait, you're serious?"

"Apparently, she thought it sounded cool." I held out the

35

cup of coffee I'd just got from the machine. "Would this help? It's fresh."

"I'm desperate for caffeine, but not *that* desperate. We've got a filter machine in the staff lounge. You want a cup?"

With Liam? Absolutely not. Spending time in his orbit was dangerous; I knew that from experience.

"I should get going."

"You drove here?"

"I rode in the ambulance, but I'll get the bus home."

"Not on Christmas Day, you won't. They stopped running an hour ago."

Oh, crap. I checked my watch, and of course he was right.

"Dammit," I muttered.

"Need a lift?"

I groaned, and Liam's face fell. Why? Surely he'd only made the offer out of obligation?

Would I be able to get a cab? If not, I'd have a long walk. How much would a cab even cost? Did they charge extra on public holidays? Probably, and I only had my emergency tenner in my pocket. Matron wouldn't be amused if I called begging for a lift at ten o'clock in the evening.

"I won't even talk." Liam gave me a tired smile, and my stomach did a backflip. "I just want you to get home safely."

What other choice did I have?

"A lift would be great," I said through gritted teeth. "Thanks."

Chapter 8

Liam was right—the coffee in the staff lounge tasted far better than the vile sludge the machine dispensed. I couldn't complain about the view while I drank it either.

As I finished the last dregs, he headed to the locker room to change out of his scrubs, and I'd have paid good money to be a fly on the wall for that show. Not that I needed to use my imagination when it came to Liam's arse. No, I had a whole bank of filthy memories, and for the millionth time, I replayed the moment when he'd dropped his trousers in front of me. Okay, both moments. And then he'd laid me on the bed and slid my skirt higher, higher, and...

"Coming?"

If only. "Yes, I'm ready."

Liam still drove the same car, the BMW, although this year, there was an empty coffee cup in every cupholder. Ever the gentleman, or at least the illusion of one, he opened the passenger door and waited for me to settle in before he took his position behind the wheel. What a difference a year made —the last time we'd been in this position, my stomach had fluttered with nervous anticipation. Now? Now, I just felt nauseated.

"Where are we going?" Liam stifled a yawn. "Do you live far from here?"

"About six miles away."

"What's your postcode?"

Once he'd programmed the satnav, he started the engine and the car purred into the night. I began a countdown—ten minutes of awkwardness, maybe fifteen if Liam drove slowly or all the traffic lights turned red. Was this better or worse than walking? On the plus side, no blisters, but on the minus side, my knickers were damp. Damn my stupid body. Why couldn't it follow my head's lead and feign indifference?

Eleven minutes and seventeen seconds passed before Liam spoke again.

"For the record, I'm incredibly sorry about last year. I didn't mean to take advantage of you. I honestly thought you were into things as much as I was."

"You didn't take advantage of me. It's fine."

"It clearly wasn't fine because when I got back with breakfast, you'd disappeared."

"Breakfast?"

"The shop along the road's always open, even on Boxing Day, so I figured I'd pick up croissants."

"I wondered where you'd gone."

"Well, it was either buy croissants or offer you soft cornflakes. The joys of being a bachelor—empty cupboards, empty fridge."

"A bachelor? Even now, you can't tell the truth."

"Huh?"

"You heard."

Liam jerked the wheel to the side and screeched to a halt in a lay-by, ignoring the annoyed honk from the car behind. The seat belt dug into my stomach. What the hell?

"What are you doing?" My voice rose an octave because this wasn't part of the plan. "Why have you stopped?"

"Tell me what you meant by that last comment."

"Oh, please. Do I have to spell it out? I wasn't upset because you screwed me senseless. I was angry because you did it behind your girlfriend's back."

"Girlfriend? What girlfriend? I didn't have a girlfriend. Hell, I *still* don't have a girlfriend."

"Then who was the woman that called?"

"What woman?"

"The one who told your answering machine she'd be round in half an hour with a special surprise? And that she wanted you in her bedroom?"

Liam's forehead crinkled, and if I hadn't known better, I'd have said he was genuinely puzzled. Then he burst out laughing.

"My sister? You're talking about my sister?"

"What?" His sister? No way. "What kind of girl talks like that to their brother?"

"The girl who brought a pecan pie over because she wanted me to assemble her new wardrobe on my day off. The more appropriate question would be 'what kind of girl goes to IKEA on Christmas Eve?'"

"But...but she sounded all...*sultry*."

"She's an actress, and when she's between TV and theatre jobs, she narrates romance novels. It's her job to sound sultry."

"I thought you had some vixen coming to visit."

"A vixen?" Liam nodded to himself. "That's not a bad description of Serena. I pity any man she gets her hands on."

What had I done? I slumped back in my seat and covered my face with my hands. This was a real roller-coaster ride. I'd gone from uncomfortable to annoyed to horrified to slightly sick in the space of thirty seconds, and all because I'd assumed the worst last year instead of waiting for Liam to show up so I could talk to him. I guess... I guess I'd just figured that the Christmas spirit had temporarily impaired his judgment, and how could he possibly want me for more than a quick roll in the sack?

"I think I've done something really, really stupid."

"For the past twelve months, I thought I'd hurt you," Liam whispered. "I tried to contact you at the retirement home, but you were never available. And when I left messages, you didn't phone me back."

"Messages? What messages? I didn't get any messages."

"A lady named Barbara promised to tell you I'd called."

I couldn't hold in my groan. "Oh, no. Barbara's got a memory like a sieve. I mean, it's so bad that she forgets to come to work at least once a month. We have a rota to remind her about the rota."

Liam let out his own pained sigh. "You mean we've lost a year? A year because of some dumb misunderstanding?"

"What do you mean, 'lost a year'? We had a one-night stand that ended in disaster." A tear popped out and rolled down the side of my nose. "*I'm* the disaster."

"A one-night stand?" I'd never forget his sweet hesitation that night, and now he had the same look. "But I never intended for it to be just one night."

"You didn't?"

"You did?"

"I have no idea what I thought! My brain was mush, okay? All I knew was that I wanted to spend time with you, so I pushed my reservations aside—I'm not normally a do-it-on-the-first-date sort of girl, by the way, or even the second—and I didn't think about the future or the rules or anything else."

"Ditto, and I'm definitely beginning to see the benefits of talking first." Liam crossed his arms over the steering wheel and rested his head on them. "If I'd known then what I know

now, I'd have waited outside the retirement home for the whole of January until I saw you."

And I'd have probably worked on the—clearly mistaken—assumption that he was a slimeball and hidden inside until he left, but it was the thought that counted.

"I've replayed that night in my head so many times."

The good parts and the bad parts. Was it better or worse to know that he hadn't cheated? Instead of wanting to kick him, now I'd be kicking myself for messing up...well...everything.

"Me too." He straightened and turned to face me. "Tell me you're not seeing anyone?"

"I've been on two dates in the last year, and they were both awful."

The first guy had suggested we go for a walk in the park, and then he'd taken me to a cemetery, and the second drank too much wine and began weeping for his ex-girlfriend. I'd ended up comforting him over dessert. *There, there it's not your fault* (it definitely was), *things will get better*. Until today, I'd ranked that night as my second-worst dating experience, but in light of new information, I bumped Crying Chris up to first place.

Liam started the engine again and peeled away from the lay-by, and this time, he drove much faster. When he pulled up outside my apartment building two minutes later, my knuckles were white.

"Where should I park?"

"Uh..." I had an assigned parking space, but I never used it. "Try around the back."

201, 202, 203... I spotted my flat number on a little plaque, and Liam abandoned the car more than parked it. Eh, that'd do. I was still fumbling with my seat belt as he yanked the passenger door open, and when I didn't climb out fast enough, he leaned in and picked me up.

"What are you doing?"

"I'm not wasting any more time."

Was this crazy? Probably, but I didn't care. Not when he hustled me into the elevator, not when he ran his hands up my thighs, and not even when the doors opened on my floor and one of my neighbours got an eyeful of my arse. Oops.

The instant my front door closed behind us, Liam slammed me up against the wood, hands everywhere. I fumbled with his belt buckle as he kissed my lips, my neck, my shoulders.

"Where's the bedroom?"

I groaned and pressed up against him, trying to get his fly undone. Why had he changed his clothes? What was wrong with the scrubs? I bet those would have come off more easily.

"The bedroom, Marissa? Unless you want me to screw you up against this door, which is always an option."

Decisions, decisions... But then the knob poked me—the *door*knob—and I pointed towards the bedroom.

"In there."

Liam picked me up again. There was nothing gentle about the way he was treating me tonight, but that didn't matter. We shared the same desperation. I needed him, and I'd take him any way I could get him.

Twice.

"I can't move."

Liam leaned over and pressed the softest kiss to the corner of my mouth. A good thing too, because after our efforts last night, my face was raw from stubble burn.

"You don't have to move."

"Somebody pinch me. Did that really happen?"

He grinned at me, blue eyes twinkling. "Did what really happen?"

"You want me to put it into actual words?"

"Yes, I think you should."

"Well, I'm not going to."

But I did lift the corner of the duvet, and yes, we were both naked. Phew. For a moment, I'd feared that I'd dreamed the whole thing.

"It's cute that you get embarrassed about sex."

"It's weird that you don't."

"Sweetheart, I was a stripper and now I'm a doctor. I've seen more body parts than I've had hot dinners. Although that isn't difficult, seeing as I eat a lot of vending-machine sandwiches."

"Why? You're not a good cook?"

"I usually take the easy option." Liam shrugged and brushed the hair away from my face. "Sorry if I was a bit rough last night. A year's worth of longing and frustration came out in one go."

"I'm not sorry at all, but I do ache in places I didn't realise I *had* places."

He trailed a finger down my side, and I squirmed under his touch. "You're ticklish?"

"Don't you dare."

"You get a pass for today." Today? Did that mean there would be a tomorrow? "I don't have to be at work until twelve, so I can spoil you until then."

Four more hours of Liam? This was the best Christmas ever. Apart from the bit where Mr. Benson broke his hip, obviously. I'd rather have avoided that incident.

"I'm yours for the spoiling. And anything else, just in case you're wondering."

"You want breakfast?" My stomach picked that moment to grumble, and Liam laughed. "I'll take that as a yes."

Despite Liam's change in career, he still had zero inhibitions. Which meant I got to enjoy the glorious sight of his bare arse as he climbed out of bed. I couldn't resist reaching out to give it a squeeze, and that earned me another smile.

"It's a yes."

He paused in the doorway. "Any requests?"

"I can't think. I literally can't think."

"Do you have eggs?"

"Yes."

"Bread?"

"Yes."

"Then you're having French toast. There's no way I'll risk going out for croissants again."

Chapter 9

L iam might have lived on sandwiches, but his fluffy French toast still put my rubbery attempts of the past to shame. Even better, he served me breakfast naked in bed, and I wasn't sure what I wanted to eat more, him or the food.

"You *can* cook. Where did you learn?"

He paused with his fork in mid-air. "My grandma taught me when I was little. We made breakfast together every Sunday."

"You're close to your family?"

"Yes, although they don't live around here anymore. My sister travels all over the place for work, my little brother's in the army, and my parents moved to Devon because they always wanted to live by the sea. How about you? Do you have family nearby?"

"Is this where we do the first-date talk?"

"If you're going to break my heart because you hate my coin collection or my cat, let's get it over with."

"You have a cat?"

"His name is Cheddar, and he adopted me last year."

Awww. "Cheddar? Let me guess... He loves cheese?"

"Yes and no. He got the name because he's a weird yellowy colour, but he's partial to Stilton. Do you have a pet?"

"No, but my parents have a cat called Marmite, and he truly does love Marmite. Which is gross, but to each their own. Uh, do you...?"

"Marmite's disgusting."

Thank goodness. "My family lives in Somerset, in a tiny village called Engleby. I'm the only one who moved away."

"Why did you move? You don't get along?"

"No, no, we get on great." I'd left Engleby because my ex got a new job, but the less said about him, the better. "I mean, my mum can be a little overpowering at times, but... I need to make an effort to see them more often."

And suddenly, the Liam mess had got a whole lot more complicated. Would we ever reach the stage where he'd want to meet my family? And if we did, how would I explain to him that they thought we'd already been dating for a year? Dammit, I was such an idiot. Why hadn't I pretended it was just a fling? A short-term mistake with an unnamed and totally unsuitable man? Stupid, dumb pride, that was why. Now Mum was planning her outfit for our wedding, and I had no idea what to do.

Liam forked up his last piece of French toast. "Family's important. You didn't go home for Christmas?"

"I had to work."

"Two years running?"

No, but I'd volunteered this year for obvious reasons.

"I swapped with Eileen. She has grandkids." And I needed to change the subject. "Shall I take the plates to the kitchen?"

"I'll do that. Then we can use those last two condoms before I go to work."

I wasn't totally sure of a condom's shelf life, but if you want an indication of how my love life usually went, the packet in my bedside table had been a week from expiring.

Luckily, Liam carried a spare in his wallet, so we'd had enough to keep ourselves amused.

"Aren't you tired?" I asked.

"Shattered, but I've survived worse. I'll take a catnap before I head in."

"Are you coming back later?"

"Am I invited?"

I quickly nodded. "I'm only sorry we lost so much time."

After Liam departed, I spent half an hour lying in bed. Boneless, exhausted, unable to move. Boy, that ceiling was really pretty.

Then a *beep* from my phone startled me, and I grabbed it off the bedside table.

Liam: Missing you already x

We'd exchanged numbers before he left. Neither of us wanted another misunderstanding, another wasted year. Three hundred and sixty-five days, three hundred and sixty-five orgasms, all down the drain.

Me: Not as much as I miss you xx

I shivered, but not from the cold. No, I was happier than I'd been in a long time, and still hot and bothered too. Liam was back. *Liam.* Once upon a time, I'd imagined screaming his name, and last night, I'd done it for real. Although I'd clapped a hand over my mouth pretty darn fast because the walls in this flat were horribly thin.

I slept—okay, daydreamed—for an hour, then dragged myself out of bed to clean the flat. If I'd known Liam would be coming home with me, I'd at least have run the vacuum cleaner around and scrubbed the shower, but better late than never. I'd also have shaved my legs because, crikey, they were hairy. He probably thought I was descended from Sasquatch. There was a reason I wore opaque tights, and it had nothing to do with fashion and everything to do with laziness. Oh, and my lady garden was more of a lady jungle. There was probably a lost species living in there. *The ivory-billed dodo, previously thought to be extinct, was today spotted by Dr. Liam Carlisle, nesting in...* Dammit, I needed scissors.

Sprucing everything up took another hour, and then I began to get twitchy. Liam hadn't texted again, and what if he changed his mind? Should I message him? Ask what time he might be back? We really needed to talk more, but he seemed to prefer using his mouth for other things. What were the rules when it came to communications? Were we meant to take it in turns? That seemed logical. And he probably hadn't texted back because he was saving someone's life.

Did all relationships start like this? With oodles of nervous energy and a burning need to check your phone every three seconds? I almost wished I were working today—at least running around at Fairfield House would keep me busy. We'd be getting ready for dinner now, setting out cutlery in the dining room and preparing trays for residents who wanted to eat in their rooms. Hmm, dinner... I could start dinner, but what on earth could I make? Apart from French toast, I had no clue what Liam liked to eat. What if he was doing Veganuary or something? Okay, it was still December, and yes, he ate eggs, but he might be vegetarian.

Sod it, I'd send him a text.

Me: Do you eat meat? x

Why wasn't he answering? Was he stitching somebody up? Or had another kid like Pharaoh come in? Or—

My phone pinged.

Liam: Yes, and I'm hoping you do too x

What did that mean? Another *ping*, a photo appeared, and

I choked on my own tongue. This wasn't the first time I'd received a dick pic, but the others had been unsolicited and utterly unimpressive. This was... Wow. Could I frame it?

Me: I think I just turned carnivore x

Which left the question of what to make for dinner. Toad-in-the-hole sprang to mind—can't think why—but I didn't have any sausages. No problem, the corner shop would be open. Nadir who ran it didn't celebrate Christmas, although he still opened an advent calendar every year. Ditto for Easter and Easter eggs.

I set out along the street, narrowly avoided getting run over because looking where I was going wasn't my strong point today, and somehow made it to the minimart alive. Nadir smiled at me from behind the counter.

"Christmas wasn't as bad as you thought it would be?"

"A miracle happened, and it turned out okay. Better than okay." Was I blushing? "I got lucky."

Ever the salesman, Nadir pointed to the lottery machine. "Then maybe today is the day to buy a ticket."

"Oh, go on then. Give me one. Lucky dip."

"Anything else?"

"I need food. Sausages and...whatever else goes into toad-in-the-hole."

"You don't know? It is a British dish, yes?"

"I'm not much of a cook."

"I will google."

The minimart might have been slightly more expensive than the big supermarket down the road, but you couldn't beat the personal service. Nadir called out the list of ingredients and I piled them into a basket, then added a lasagne from the "dinner for two" section just in case it all went wrong. And a trifle, because I figured we'd work it off later.

As I passed the stationery section, I picked out a "Get well soon" card, a box of chocolates, and a puzzle book for Mr. Benson. If he hadn't tripped, I'd never have ended up with Liam again, so I certainly owed him a few treats.

Nadir grinned as he took the items out of my basket. "Meals for two and a smile. You are having a date, yes?"

My smile got wider. "I am."

"If he mentions another girl, this time you should leave before dessert."

"I will, but he seems really normal."

"That's what Jules from the hair salon said about her date last week, and then he left early because his wife's car broke down."

"His *wife*?"

Nadir shrugged. "Jules says that fifty percent of the men on the Tinder are snakes. Twenty-seven pounds thirty-five."

At home, I prepped dinner and watched two episodes of *Miranda*, and there was still no word from Liam. Did I have time to go to the hospital and give Mr. Benson his gifts? I'd checked the bus timetable, and the number sixty-four was still running. If Liam saw me, would he think I was stalking him?

Not if I messaged him first.

Me: Coming to visit Mr. Benson x

And okay, maybe I hoped for a glimpse of Liam as well...

Chapter 10

I t wasn't every day that I wore lipstick to visit the Darwin ward, but needs must.

"Is that a box of Quality Street?"

Mr. Benson's eyes lit up when he spotted the chocolates. They were his favourite, even if the toffees did stick to his dentures. He'd suck on them for hours. Which left me with the orange and strawberry creams, but that was okay—fruit was good for you, right?

"Yes, and I brought you a crossword book too."

"Are you going to help me with the tricky clues?"

"I can stay for a bit."

At Fairfield House, we did puzzles together a couple of times a week, usually on my lunch breaks. Anything was better than watching *Homes Under the Hammer* or another episode of *Bargain Hunt*, which many of our residents were fans of because they remembered all the antiques from the first time around. And at least today, the crossword would help to distract me from...

"Hard. Four letters, sounds like something you put on your foot," Mr. Benson read out.

Dammit, Marissa. Do not go there.

"Rock. Try 'rock.'"

"That fits." Mr. Benson's gaze flitted past me. "Oh, good evening, Dr. Carlisle."

Liam was here? My heart sped up, and I craned my head back to find him looking down at me.

"Uh, hi."

He smiled and raised an eyebrow. "Crossword puzzles?"

"It's our little ritual."

"Always good to give your mind a workout. Time for your medication, Mr. Benson."

The old man winked at me. "It's worth coming to this place just for the pills. Some of the nurses aren't too bad either."

"You need to behave yourself."

"I get leeway for being over eighty."

Liam chuckled as he made notes on the chart. "Mr. Benson, if I have your body at eighty, I'll be a happy man." Then he leaned down and whispered in my ear, "Yours too."

Oh. My. Goodness.

Mr. Benson swallowed his pills and picked up his puzzle book again, mercifully oblivious to the other conversation taking place.

"Sounds a bit like a water bird and makes you happy. Eight letters, starts with G."

Liam snorted quietly as he moved on to the next patient.

Grrr. "Good luck."

"Thank you, love, but what's the answer?"

"Good luck. That's the answer. It rhymes with 'duck.'"

"Oh, yes." Mr. Benson filled in the boxes. "You're great at these."

Barely a minute passed before my phone buzzed.

Liam: Cock. The first word is cock, Marissa. You got the second one wrong too.

Me: Maybe you could help me to correct my mistakes later?

Liam: I intend to. Always good to give your body a workout as well ;) x

In the past, I'd never been a fan of exercise, but a girl reserved the right to change her mind, didn't she?

Me: Can you recommend a good cardio instructor? Xx

Liam: He'll pick you up right after his shift x

That evening, the atmosphere in Liam's BMW was heated rather than frosty. He ran his hand up my thigh before we left the car park, and that kiss he gave me when he climbed in? My lips still stung from the intensity, and my knickers had practically melted. Were calloused lips a thing? Probably I should ask a doctor about that.

"Mind if we swing by my place first?" he asked. "I need to pick up some clothes."

Aw, I'd kind of hoped he wasn't planning to wear any. "Sure."

"Or we can stay there. Your choice."

"I already started making dinner."

"Then we'll make it a flying visit. I haven't been shopping all week, and you probably cook better than I do."

"If I follow a recipe, I can rustle up an edible meal. But don't put yourself down—your French toast was delicious."

"I can only do breakfast. French toast, eggs, bacon, pancakes, sausages. With or without ketchup."

"I love pancakes."

He reached over and squeezed my hand. "Then guess what you're getting for breakfast tomorrow?"

Traffic near the hospital was heavier than yesterday,

probably due to the time of day, but we soon cleared the jams and headed into the suburbs. The houses got bigger and less familiar. Neatly trimmed trees lined the streets, and cars were tucked away on driveways rather than being parked at the kerb. This was the posh part of town, and I might not have paid much attention during the trip to Liam's flat last year, but I could have sworn he lived in the opposite direction.

"Did you move?"

He kept his eyes on the road but grinned. "My previous occupation left me with a nice house deposit."

"Nice" was an understatement. Liam pulled into the driveway of a large detached house on a quiet street and parked under the bare boughs of an old tree. An oak, perhaps? A security light blinked on, and *wow*. The double-fronted Victorian was my dream home. When I was a teenager, I used to doodle pictures of my perfect house, and they'd always looked remarkably similar to this. Well, apart from the builder's skip sitting on the lawn.

Liam turned the engine off. "I moved in eight months ago. The place still needs work, and I'm doing as much as I can myself to save money. But at least it's connected to the outside world. My old flat had no cell signal, and the broadband speed was rubbish."

"It's beautiful."

"No, it's well built. You're beautiful."

Smooth, Liam, smooth. Much smoother than his cheek was, anyway. He'd gone past a five o'clock shadow, and the stubble scratched my palm as I ran a hand over it.

"Uh, would you mind picking up a razor too? My chin hasn't quite recovered from yesterday." Or my inner thighs, but that was too much information.

"Give me my way, and it never will. You want to see inside?"

"Ooh, yes."

I'd quite happily help with the renovations too, but it was far too soon to offer, wasn't it? DIY wasn't my forte, but I'd watched enough property shows on TV that I knew my hammer from my chisel. And I could paint a wall. When I was younger, I'd helped Dad to decorate the whole of the house, and there were hardly any drips.

Liam swung open the front door and flicked on the light, giving me the chance to take in the decor in the hallway. Lovely. He'd done it out in pale green with a white side table, a low leather sofa, and a half-naked woman standing by the staircase.

Hold on...

What?

Chapter 11

"Surprise!" The woman turned on a fifty-megawatt smile. "Happy Christmas."

Should I avert my gaze? Scratch her eyes out? Slap Liam? Run?

Mind boggled, I settled for staring open-mouthed. She'd gone to town with the hairspray, and the only thing preserving her modesty was a strategically placed pink gift-bow.

Liam recovered first. "Kirsten, what are you doing here?"

"Waiting for you, of course. Where were you last night?"

"That's none of your business."

"Of course it's my business. I had to sleep alone." Her eyes narrowed. "Were you with *her*?"

I wriggled out of Liam's grasp. "Maybe I'll leave you guys to it."

"You're not going anywhere. Not again."

Oh, really? Well, I might have made a mistake last year with his sister, but unless his family was spectacularly liberal, the floozy standing in the hallway wasn't a relative. And that meant I'd been made a fool of yet again. I stumbled backwards and nearly fell down the steps in my haste to escape, and I didn't even know where I was. This was the good part of town, and the only time I ventured over here was when I accidentally got on the wrong bus.

Left or right?

Left or right?

I picked left. After all, I was never right. Just wrong, wrong, wrong. Wrong job, wrong man, wrong bloody life. And I needed to go to the gym. I could barely breathe, my calves were on fire, and I hadn't even made it to the corner yet.

Footsteps pounded along the pavement behind me, and an arm snaked around my waist, stopping me in my tracks. Liam's hot breath puffed against my ear. Of course, *he* didn't sound like a steam train on its last legs. That was all me.

"Marissa, don't run. Please. I'll explain."

I twisted in his grip and stuck my hands on my hips. "Oh, fantastic. I'm dying to hear this one."

"Just come back to the house. Give me ten minutes, and then you can leave if you want to. I'll even drive you home."

Tears ran down my cheeks as he led me along the pavement. The house I'd thought was so beautiful the first time I saw it now took on a foreboding air as he pushed open the front door.

This time, the woman was sitting on the couch, but she rose when we walked in, reaching for Liam. Great, the gift-bow had fallen off.

He didn't let go of my hand as he pointed at the door.

"Kirsten, get out. Now."

"How can you say that? And how could you cheat on me? With *her*?" A tear escaped from the corner of her eye, and she smeared mascara across her cheek when she wiped it away. "I've always been here for you."

She took another step towards us, and I inched backwards, but Liam wouldn't let me go. This was beyond awkward.

"Look, I can't be here," I told him.

He gripped my hand tighter. "Please, just a few minutes."

Then he turned back to Kirsten, and his expression hardened. "How did you get in?"

"With my key, of course." She held it up, dangling on a heart-shaped keyring.

"Get dressed and leave. You're breaching your restraining order again, and in thirty seconds, I'm calling the police."

Restraining order? What restraining order? Why did I get the feeling I was missing vital parts of the Liam jigsaw?

Kirsten pouted at him. "Why do you always do this? *Why*? We were made for each other."

"Because you're delusional."

"Have you been talking to my psychiatrist? Because she said that too, but she just doesn't understand." Kirsten dropped to her knees in front of Liam and wrapped her arms around his leg. "Why can't you see that we're perfect together?"

He bent to pry her hands away, and she tried to kiss him. Okay, maybe he was right and she *was* a raving lunatic? This definitely wasn't normal. Every time he pulled one hand away, she grabbed him with the other, all the time pleading and crying and wailing.

Which left me with a decision to make.

Should I run again, or should I fight? My whole life, I'd made the easy choices, but was Liam worth battling for? Was what we had together worth the effort? I thought back to last night... Our time together hadn't just been spectacularly amazing in an orgasmic way, it had been comfortable too. Liam was sweet and kind and easy to talk to, plus he made great French toast.

Hell yes, he was worth the effort.

So I snatched a cushion off the couch and used it to wallop Kirsten.

"Get away from him!"

She finally let go of his arm but turned on me instead, talons out. "You little..."

That gave Liam the opening he needed. He clamped his arms around her waist, carried her out the door, and dumped her at the bottom of the steps. I had the presence of mind to snatch her coat off the arm of the couch and throw it after her.

Liam moved to close the door, but I stopped him.

"Wait." I hurried down the steps and retrieved the key from Kirsten's hand, then ran back inside. "Okay, I'm done."

He slammed the door, and I sank onto the couch. My legs were jelly now.

"What just happened?"

Liam sat next to me and took my hand. "I was planning to tell you, but last night didn't seem like the right time to start discussing my stalker."

I had to concede that was true.

"How the heck did you end up with her?"

"I couldn't get you out of my head, so I decided to take drastic measures."

"Involving what? A visit to the asylum?"

He groaned. "Kind of. Tinder."

I couldn't help it—I had to laugh. Seemed as if half of the women on there were snakes too.

"We went on three dates, and Kirsten seemed reasonably normal. Two weeks later, I had to go to my cousin's graduation party, and she offered to feed Cheddar while I was away. I got back and found she'd moved into my house."

My eyes bugged out. "Like, she'd slept here every night?"

"Like she'd hung all her clothes in the closet, repainted the lounge, and got her mail redirected."

"Holy cow."

"She followed me everywhere for weeks. Management banned her from the hospital, so she sat in the car park every day and waited for me to leave. But I hadn't seen her for over a month." Liam blew out a long breath. "I thought she'd finally moved on to some other poor schmuck."

"I don't know what to say."

"I'll call the police tomorrow and ask them to have a word. Another one."

A horrible thought struck me. "Did you and she ever..."

He understood what I was asking and laid his forehead against mine. "No, I swear. Usually I'm a gentleman. You're the only woman who's made me jump into bed like that on a first date."

"Date?" I teased, trying to make light of the situation.

"Okay, so I haven't taken you on a proper date yet, but I'll make up for it. I'll take you anywhere. Name the place."

"Bora-Bora?"

"Let's save that one for the honeymoon. Maybe somewhere a little closer to home?"

Wait, did he just say what I thought he said? Or were my ears playing tricks on me?

"Uh..." Words. Lost. "Honeymoon?"

"One day," he whispered. "Not yet."

Not yet. Not yet for what? A date? Or a bloody wedding? Liam Carlisle confused the heck out of me.

Then his lips touched mine, and I realised I didn't care.

We never did get to my flat that night. Liam rummaged around in the freezer and found a pizza, and we shared it along with a bottle of wine on the squashy sofa in the lounge. I only hoped Kirsten hadn't contaminated it with her scrawny backside.

"Is there anything else I should know about you?" I asked.

"Do you have any more sisters? Or another harlot hell-bent on clawing her way into your bed?"

"Well, you already know about the stripping, so I guess that saves us one interesting conversation. Plus I got tied naked to a lamp post at my brother's stag do. That occasionally comes up, but there aren't any other skeletons lurking."

"A lamp post? How on earth did that happen?"

"Alcohol. How else?"

"I wish I'd seen that."

"I'm sure he'll show you the photos if you ask him nicely."

Was Liam being serious? Did he want me to meet his family someday? Or was it another flippant comment like the honeymoon one? Relationships were a minefield, and I had to tread carefully because I did *not* want to blow this one up. So I giggled in case it was a joke.

Liam just grinned back at me. "Or I can demonstrate right now, if you like? I'm pretty sure I've got a pair of handcuffs left over from my act. Fancy arresting me, Officer Marissa?"

"Do you still have the uniform?"

"Want me to put it on?"

I nodded. "And then I want you to take it off."

"We never did finish the grand tour." When he stood, his crotch was at my eye level, and I saw he was hard already. "Let me show you the bedroom."

On second thoughts, perhaps we could skip the whole uniform part?

"Lead the way."

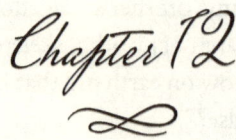

Chapter 12

My bicycle was still padlocked to a drainpipe at Fairfield House, so Liam drove me home to change in the morning and then took me to work. Oh, I could get used to that. Riding in his car was so much more civilised than dodging potholes on two wheels.

"I'll see you tonight?" I asked.

Liam worked shifts, but earlier over breakfast—pancakes, as promised—he'd said he would finish at four today. Our plans were tentative, but he'd mentioned dinner.

"I'll pick you up from your flat at six."

"We're going to your place?"

"No, I'm taking you on a date."

A proper date? This week got better and better. "Where?"

"It's a surprise."

"Can I have a tiny clue?"

"No."

"Aw, come on. I won't know what to wear otherwise."

"Okay, I haven't decided where I'm taking you yet, but I promise you'll love it. And dress up."

Liam touched his lips to mine, then deepened the kiss. His

arms tightened around me, and not for the first time this week, I wondered if I was dreaming the whole thing. Liam was way, way out of my league, not only in terms of hotness but in social status too. He was a freaking doctor. I was a nobody.

"Why are you here?" I blurted.

His brow creased. "Because you needed a ride to work?"

"No, I mean here with me? You could have any woman you wanted."

"That's not true, but even if it were, I'd still choose you."

"But why?"

"Because you're cute as hell and you don't even realise it. Because you're sweet and patient, even when an old gal asks you the same question six times in five minutes. Because last year, you didn't judge me for being a stripper to make ends meet. Because you're not with me now just because I'm a doctor and you want to brag to your friends. Because you whacked Kirsten with a cushion." He ran his hands down my arms and locked his gaze on mine. "Want me to carry on?"

"Uh, that's okay."

"So, why are you here with me?"

"Are you kidding?"

"I wouldn't kid about something so important."

He really was serious, wasn't he? But I wasn't eloquent. I couldn't reel off a whole list of qualities.

"Because...because you're *Liam*. And every time you come near me, my heart beats out of my chest."

"As a doctor, I can tell you that's not physically possible."

"Well, my nipples definitely go hard." I clapped both hands over my mouth. "Sorry, sorry! I didn't mean to say that. Uh, I think you're kind and clever and easy to talk to. And also forgiving of my social ineptitude."

He just laughed. "Six o'clock. Don't be late."

The day went soooooo slowly. I daydreamed about Liam while I changed the beds, then rehashed every word he'd ever said to me while I sorted the laundry. Even giving Mr. Mattheson a sponge bath couldn't dampen my mood.

"You look happy, dear," Mrs. Simpkins said. "Did you get a nice present from Santa?"

"Oh, yes. Quite a few, in fact."

"That's lovely. William gave me socks again. He ordered them on the internet."

William was Mr. Benson—we always called residents by their surnames out of politeness, staff rules—and when Mrs. Simpkins tilted a foot so I could admire her gift, I saw a cartoon woman doing something rather suggestive with a pair of Christmas puddings.

"They look very, uh, festive."

"They're warm, too. William's ever such a gentleman. Some of the ladies and I have been knitting him a chess set— would you take it into the hospital for him?"

A knitted chess set? I dreaded to think. Still, it was better than the crocheted Noah's ark they'd attempted the year before last. But who was Mr. Benson meant to play chess with? Me? Because I didn't know my knight from my pawn, and I usually lost at noughts and crosses.

"Of course I will."

I was never normally a clock-watcher, but today I couldn't keep my eyes off the time. At five o'clock on the dot, I sped home for a shower. Should I wear trousers? A skirt? In the end, I settled on a plain black dress, an outfit I'd bought two years ago for Mrs. Garner's hundredth-birthday bash. She loved old black-and-white movies, so we'd decided on an old-school Hollywood theme, but she'd breathed her last two weeks before the big day and the dress had sat in my wardrobe ever since. I snipped off the tag and wriggled into it, added a swipe of mascara plus a coat of lip gloss, and then I was ready. Make-up wasn't really my thing, nor any other kind of beauty treatment, not after the fake-tan incident early last year. I'd only wanted a bit of colour, and yes, I'd certainly got it, but tangerine wasn't quite what I'd had in mind. Mr. Benson, ever the joker, had bought all the residents sunglasses, and I'd decided to embrace my pasty whiteness for the rest of my days.

I was watching out the window when Liam's car drew up in my parking space right on time, and he tapped the entry buzzer a minute later.

"Good to go?" he asked as I opened the door.

"I'll just grab my bag." I took in his suit. "Is this outfit okay? Am I underdressed?"

He looked me up and down so slowly, so intensely, that my blood heated under his gaze. Holy global warming.

"No, you're overdressed."

"But I'm literally wearing one thing. Well, unless you count my knickers, but those don't show." I'd even checked for VPL in the mirror. "Is it the earrings? Should I take them off? They're only cubic zirconia."

Liam stepped closer, backing me up against the wall. Ooh, he'd put on aftershave, but it did nothing to mask the pheromones that oozed from his pores. When he kissed his way up my jaw, I sagged into his arms.

"I thought we were going out?"

"First, we're coming in."

"Huh?"

He grazed his fingertips over my thighs, and thank goodness I'd shaved my legs.

"Let's be fashionably late."

By the time we staggered out to the car half an hour later, I'd already eaten dessert. My hair was a mess, and I'd been forced to do a hasty repair job on my lip gloss, but Liam's dimples were out in full force.

"You're a little minx," he whispered as he helped me into the passenger seat. "Where did you learn to do that thing with your tongue? Actually, forget it. I don't want to know."

"*Dirty* magazine."

My guilty secret. The women's monthly that promised to teach you everything you'd never admit to wanting to know.

"I'll buy you a subscription."

My turn to grin. "No need; I already have one."

Liam had booked a table for two at an upmarket restaurant I'd never have dared to walk into alone, complete with candles, an actual pianist, and a waiter who pulled my chair out so I could sit down.

"This is lovely."

"There weren't many options with only a day's notice, and half the places are on limited service after Christmas."

"We could be eating kebabs on a park bench, and I'd still be thrilled. Or I guess Happy Meals would be more appropriate because...you know... Never mind. I'll stop talking now."

Liam reached across the table and took my hands in his.

"Getting booked to strip for the old guys was the best thing that ever happened to me."

"I preferred the evening entertainment."

"You've got me every evening from now on, you realise that? Unless I'm working nights. And if I'm working nights, I'll be making you breakfast."

"I…" I didn't know what to say. A fist pump would be inappropriate, right? "I…"

My phone rang before I could formulate a coherent response. Why hadn't I put the bloody thing on silent? Everyone turned to stare at me as I fumbled through my handbag, hunting for a device that was clearly in there but which didn't want to be found. Damn my mother and her impeccable sense of timing. I knew it was her because Frank Sinatra was singing "My Way" and that was her favourite song, plus the residents at Fairfield House liked it too, and… Ah, there it was. *Reject, reject, reject.* But Mum didn't take the hint and called straight back again.

"Do you need to get that?"

"It's my mum."

"Family's important," Liam reminded me. "And if she's anything like my mum, she'll never give up."

Wasn't that the truth? When I answered, she began speaking before I even got a chance to say hello.

"I've discussed it with the rest of the family, and we've decided to move Christmas dinner to New Year's Eve instead of New Year's Day so you can come. Isn't that wonderful?"

"Yes, but—"

"Don't tell me you have to work after all?"

"Uh, well…"

Mum gave a long sigh. "If this is about that Liam, we all know he's not real. It was sweet of you to avoid hurting Richie Harris's feelings, but there's no need to keep pretending with your family."

Oh, sheesh. A week ago, that would have been good news. Horribly embarrassing, but good news. I could have swallowed my pride, taken the train to Somerset, and enjoyed turkey and stuffing. But now? *Super* awkward. Mum had called my bluff on the New-Year's-Day-wedding-rehearsal excuse, then called me out on my lies, and I was running out of options.

Well played, Mum. Well played.

"Can I think about this and call you back?"

"What is there to think about?"

"I'm a little busy right now."

"But this is important, Marissa. You've been avoiding us for a year, and it feels as if we're losing you. Did we do something wrong? Did *I* do something wrong?"

"No, no, you didn't." Crap, I'd screwed up so much worse than I thought. "You didn't do anything wrong, but I'm on a date, so could I just—"

Liam jumped at the sound of her shriek, and my ears began ringing. Even the waiter two tables over looked around sharply.

"Tell me everything!"

"Mum, *I'm on a date.*"

"You're right, you're right. What was I thinking? Call me in an hour and tell me everything. Who's the lucky man? Do you have photos?"

"I'm hanging up now."

"You'll be bringing him for Christmas dinner, won't you? New Year's dinner, I mean. There's plenty of room, and your father bought a turkey big enough to feed us twice over."

"Please, just leave me alone."

"One hour. Call me."

I shut the phone off completely and dropped it back in my handbag. The other diners had gone back to their conversations, but Liam was chuckling as he pretended to read the menu.

"It's not funny. This is my life."

"Oh, come on. I get a psycho stalker, and you have a mother who's turned nosiness into an art form."

A groan escaped. "She's probably picking out names for her grandchildren as we speak."

"My mother keeps a list on the fridge. My sister refuses to ruin her figure, and my brother's getting divorced, so I'm feeling the pressure."

I dropped my head into my hands. "Can we get wine?"

"Hey, it's not that bad. I'm twenty-four, so I figure we've got a year or two before she starts knitting baby outfits."

Baby outfits? What? My brain was struggling to process everything. *We've* got a year or two?

"It's...it's not that."

"Then what is it?"

"Mum wants to move our family get-together to New Year's Eve."

"Are you working that day?"

"No, and that's why she's moving it. I just don't want to go."

"Why not? You said you get on well and you need to see them more often, so there's your chance."

"Because she wants you to go too, which is super awkward. I mean, this is only our first proper date, and we barely know each other, and..."

I trailed off, hoping he'd be working or have a family engagement of his own planned. Or a party, or a vacation, or even a freaking court appearance. But no such luck.

"I know it's soon, but I'd love to go with you."

"Mum'll interrogate you the second you walk through the door."

"I promise not to mention the stripping or the stalker. Or the handcuffs."

Oh, the handcuffs. I'd never watch a cop show in the same way again.

"Honestly, I can make an excuse. Somerset's a long way."

"I'll drive. It'll be faster than taking public transport." He squeezed my hand. "Marissa, what's wrong? What's the problem?"

I sucked in a breath. "This is so humiliating."

"Last night, we walked into my house and found a naked woman in the hallway. What could be worse than that?"

I cringed behind my menu as the whole sorry story came tumbling out. Patty Harris, Richie, my tiny fib about a doctor named Liam, the way my lies had snowballed and spun out of control... The waiter hovered for a while, then left because Liam was laughing too hard to order.

"So, let me get this straight. You told your mother we were dating for a year, but we weren't, and now she thinks we aren't dating, but we are?"

"That's about right."

"You couldn't make it up."

"Well, technically I did."

The corners of Liam's eyes crinkled. "If you used me as your imaginary boyfriend, that must mean you liked me."

"I thought you were a cheating git."

"But you still liked me. C'mon, admit it."

"There were parts that I liked."

Such as the taut, hard muscles and the equipment he'd mastered to a gold standard.

"Parts? Which parts?"

"Shut up."

"No, this is fun. Which parts?"

"Fine, I liked you, okay? The whole package. And you can wipe that smug smile off your face."

He didn't.

"So, are you going to call your mum back and tell her we're coming?"

"I guess. What about the whole charade?"

"We'll just have to spend a lot of time between now and New Year's Eve getting to know each other, won't we?"

I took a deep breath. "I might also have inadvertently dragged your sister into this mess as well. Mum thinks we're attending her wedding rehearsal on New Year's Day. That was my first excuse when Mum originally tried to move Christmas dinner, and now obviously the two of them can never meet because—"

Liam just laughed. "Relax. Serena will play along."

"She will?"

"My sister loves drama. Telling your mum she changed her mind at the rehearsal dinner will be nothing for Serena."

"I... Uh... Are you sure?"

"She still owes me a favour for assembling that wardrobe. Shall we order now?"

Could it really be that easy? "Yes, we should order."

This was the dream I never wanted to wake up from.

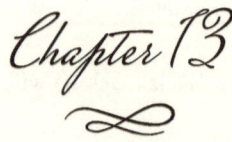

Chapter 13

"So, we met in a wine bar?" Liam confirmed.

"Yes, at the end of last November. I was drinking a pina colada; you had red wine."

"I'm not a fan of red wine."

"Ah, crap. I told my mum you loved it."

He glanced across at me from the driver's seat. "You got pretty far with this whole fantasy thing, didn't you?"

I gave his thigh a squeeze. "Can you blame me?"

That earned me a kiss at the next set of traffic lights. "Guess not. Anything else I should know about my tastes?"

"Tell me you prefer rugby to football?"

"I do."

"Thank goodness for that."

We'd planned to discuss all these things earlier in the week, but every time we started discussing our fake relationship, we got distracted by the real one. Unfortunately—or fortunately, depending on how you looked at it—we were still at the tear-each-other's-clothes-off-at-every-opportunity stage, and although *Dirty* magazine said it was just a phase, I couldn't see it ending any time soon. At least the two-hour car journey to

Somerset gave us time to play twenty questions. Liam even knew how old I was now.

"It's the white cottage up here on the right," I told him as we got near.

"Nice garden."

"My dad has green fingers."

Liam turned into the driveway and parked beside my dad's Renault. Had we prepped well enough? Only time would tell.

"Ready?" he asked.

"I'm never ready for my mother."

He popped the boot and took out our overnight bags. I'd offered for us to stay in a hotel, but Mum wouldn't hear of it. My parents had bought their house when property was affordable, which meant they had three spare bedrooms ready for guests who rarely came. And the nearest hotel was ten miles away. Mabel Truscott ran a B&B in the village, but Mabel was a world-class busybody, and I'd rather sleep in the car than fuel the local gossip mill.

"Will your mum put us in separate rooms?" Liam had asked when I gave him the news. "Mine would. She's old-fashioned that way."

"I thought she was desperate for grandkids?"

"The stork brings those. At least, that's what she's always claimed."

"Is she a bit...uh..."

"Prudish? Yeah. Sex ed was a real eye-opener, let me tell you, and for crying out loud, don't mention the stripping or my brother's stag do in front of her."

"I swear my lips are sealed. And we'll both be in my room. My mum's quite liberal that way. Plus she also wants more grandkids, so our parents have that much in common."

"Then you'd better keep the noise down."

I'd tried to stay quiet during the week, truly I had, but my neighbour still knocked on the wall twice. At that point, I'd packed a bag, and we'd headed for Liam's place. An emergency locksmith had changed all the locks, plus Liam had fitted bolts to the doors just in case Kirsten got any more ideas. He'd also cleared out half his closet and made space for my stuff in the bathroom cabinet. This was serious, wasn't it? I wasn't sure whether to be ecstatic or terrified.

And now we were about to move our fledgling relationship another step forward.

As we walked up the path to the front door, Liam leaned closer and whispered, "Did you remember the gag?"

"Shhh." I raised my hand to knock, but my fist hit empty air.

"Marissa!" Mum yanked me into a hug so fast I got whiplash, and then she tossed me aside just as quickly. "And you must be Liam."

Poor guy. His eyes bulged as she squashed the life out of him, and before he got his breath back, she grabbed his hand and dragged him into the house. Well, I had warned him.

"Hi, Dad."

He gave me a little wave from the hall, then retreated to the safety of the lounge. My nephews were in there already, wreaking havoc.

Mum turned around and pulled my sleeve. "Let's put your things in your room, then you can come and have a nice glass of wine. Liam, we've bought a nice burgundy for you. Marissa said it's your favourite."

"Sorry," I mouthed at him.

"Good thing I love you," he mouthed back as she pulled him up the stairs.

What?

Did he just say what I thought he said? Or were my lip-reading skills as poor as my lying ones?

I was still puzzling-slash-freaking out when Mum flung open the door to my old bedroom. My parents didn't need the

74

space, so they'd barely touched it over the years. Rosettes from childhood horse shows decorated my corkboard, and trophies I'd won for junior gymnastics sat on the shelf above my desk. Don't be too impressed—I'd won "Most Spectacular Tumble" in both disciplines, three years running. But the training hadn't gone completely to waste—only yesterday, Liam had congratulated me on my flexibility, although my coordination still left a lot to be desired.

"I bought you a few bits and pieces." Mum winked as she backed out of the room. "Have fun, kids."

No. She didn't. Tell me she didn't.

Liam walked over to my bedside table and picked up the first box. "Ribbed, for your pleasure?"

"Sometimes, I hate my mother."

He grinned, and he grinned wide. "I love your mother. Lube *and* a bottle of champagne? She's really spoiling us."

"Can I just sink through the floor?"

"Nope. Look, she's even tied mistletoe to the light fixture." Liam wasn't kidding—there was an actual bush hanging from the ceiling. He dropped the box he was holding and held out a hand. "Come here."

My brain was still catching up with reality. "What did you say on the stairs?"

"That I love you?"

"But...but...we've only been seeing each other for a week."

Liam wrapped me up in his arms. "You've been living in my head for a year, and when you know, you know. Shit, does that sound creepy?"

Sudden? Yes. But not creepy, and was it really any weirder than my fake-boyfriend stunt? Deep down, had my subconscious known he was the man for me?

"I... I..."

"Don't worry; I don't expect you to say it back. Not yet, anyway."

"I'm so glad I decided to work the last two Christmas Days."

"Me too." His smile softened, and my heart skipped. "Shall we test out that mistletoe?"

"That sounds—"

"Marissa!" Mum's voice echoed up the stairs. "If you're finished playing with Liam, could you help to peel the potatoes?"

"Uh, rain check?"

Liam laughed. "Guess we've been summoned. Come on, let's do the family thing. We need to practise."

Did he mean...?

He was already halfway down the stairs, and I ran to catch up with him. "What did—?"

"Shhh." He put a finger to my lips. "Later, beautiful."

"Urgh. I ate way too much."

I tried to stretch out my feet in front of the sofa, but one of my nephews was sitting in the way. Liam tightened his arm around my shoulders. Dinner was over, and he hadn't run screaming into the night despite my dad's terrible jokes, so I had to take that as a good sign.

"You've burned plenty of calories over the past week," Liam whispered, his lips brushing my ear. "And I'm a big fan of your curves."

"Is it bedtime yet?"

"Eight o'clock."

I groaned. Four hours until the clock struck midnight. Four hours before we could legitimately make our escape without everyone knowing exactly what we planned to get up to. Could I feign some sort of illness? Would that work? We couldn't even have a lie-in tomorrow seeing as we were going to Liam's sister's fake wedding rehearsal. Yes, yes, I should have come clean about that, but firstly, I was a massive chicken, and secondly, I could avoid the traditional after-Christmas walk if I skipped out early. Dad's favourite route had a *lot* of hills, and last time, I'd sprained my ankle in a rabbit hole.

"Is it time to open the rest of the presents?" my brother-in-law asked. He looked ready for bed as well, but that was mainly because he'd drunk most of the wine, as usual.

Liam had got through a glass and a half of burgundy to keep my mother happy, then switched to water, but my brother-in-law wasn't about to pass up free drinks. No, Steven had polished off the rest of the bottle and then moved on to Dad's whisky. It was Liam who'd taken on the task of entertaining my nephews, and he'd graciously lost at Scalextric, then answered a hundred questions about being a doctor. He didn't even mind when the kids started calling him "Uncle Liam," which was all kinds of sweet.

Meanwhile, Mum had polished off three glasses of rosé—or was it four?—and she was sitting on the floor with a puzzle, one of those plastic boxes and a bunch of coloured blocks that were meant to fit inside, Tetris-style.

"I don't know how kids can possibly do these things. They're impossible."

The nearest nephew stuffed the bricks into the box and handed it back to her five seconds later.

"Like this, Grandma."

She studied it, eyes unfocused. "Ah. Let's open those presents, shall we?"

"Wait, wait." My bookworm of a sister finally put down her novel and grabbed the TV remote. "It's time for the lottery draw."

"I actually bought a ticket," I said, although it was stuck to the fridge at home, and I couldn't remember the numbers. "Nadir from the minimart talked me into it."

Liam nuzzled my neck. "I've already won the lottery this week."

I lowered my voice to a whisper. "Keep that up, and you'll get lucky again later."

"I'll keep something else up too."

"Any chance there could be an emergency at the hospital right now?"

"Nice try. This is fun."

"I can think of something more fun."

"We're going to have a very happy New Year."

In front of the TV, my sister ripped up her lottery tickets and shoved them into a rubbish bag already half filled with wadded-up wrapping paper. Guess this wasn't her lucky week.

"Well, that was a waste of money. Life sucks."

Secretly, I'd always hoped that Janie would win a million so she could finally start to enjoy life. At the moment, she spent every day running around after her kids and her husband, who was basically a giant man-child himself. Was I a terrible person for disliking her choice in men? Steven had been vaguely charming when they first met, but after they said "I do," he'd given up trying, as if buying a wedding band excused him from any kind of housework or DIY for the rest of time. If I won the jackpot, I'd take Janie on holiday and hire somebody to clean her house.

"Don't be sad, dear," Mum said. "We're here with family, and that's the most important thing. Marissa, could you pass out the presents?"

"Sure, Mum."

My dad had outdone himself again, with a box of chocolates from the petrol station for me and a car air freshener for my sister. He'd obviously forgotten once again that she didn't drive. Oh, she'd taken lessons, but tests freaked her out, and she got so nervous sitting beside the examiner that she'd failed six times. Janie rode a moped, and like me, she was well-acquainted with the bus timetable.

Liam got a can of motor oil. The good kind, my dad was at pains to point out—fully synthetic for extended performance.

"Thanks," Liam said. "That's really useful."

"It's sweet of you to pretend," I whispered.

"Don't want to upset my future father-in-law."

"Are you joking? You're joking, right?"

Liam wrapped both arms around me and drew me close. "You'll just have to stick around and find out, won't you?"

Could he feel my heart hammering against my ribcage? "You won't get rid of me in a hurry. As long as there are no more naked girls, anyway."

"Cross my heart. Your heart."

"You're too damn sweet, Liam Carlisle."

"Back at you, Marissa..." His cheeks turned pink. "Uh, I'm not sure I ever got your surname?"

Oops. "It's Taylor."

"Taylor-Carlisle. That'll do."

"Don't you ever stop?"

"Nope. Does that bother you?"

"Can't say it does."

Even though I'd tried to deny it, Liam and Mum were right. Spending time with my family was fun, Steven excepted, and with Liam beside me, my heart was full. Things might have moved fast between us, but this relationship felt as if it was meant to be. Fate, kismet, destiny, call it what you like, but something had pushed us together—twice—and now I couldn't imagine being apart.

When Big Ben chimed on the television and the new year began, I made a silent wish: Please let every Christmas be as happy as this one.

And please let me have fireworks later.

If you enjoyed this book...

The next book in the Happy Ever After series is Serena's story, *A Very Happy Valentine*...

To go or not to go, that is the question...

School reunions suck, everyone knows this, but Serena Carlisle has put herself down as a "maybe." Maybe she'll stay home and cry into her ice cream, or maybe she'll put on her big-girl pants and show her old classmates that she's managed to make something of herself.

Marc di Gregorio is Hollywood's hottest property, and Serena's getting paid to kiss him on stage every night. A dream job, right? It would be if not for Owen Cadwallader, the man she last saw eight years ago as she was loaded into the back of a police car at the school prom. The teenage crush she's never been able to forget. He's a "maybe" too, but will Serena manage to hold her nerve and face him again? Or should she take the easy option and drown her sorrows with a handsome heartthrob instead?

For more details:

www.elise-noble.com/hv

And if you like romcoms, you might also like my Trouble series, starting with *Trouble in Paradise*.

When Callie Shawcross's fiancé jilts her days before the wedding, her best friend insists a relaxing break in the sleepy Egyptian town of Fidda Hilal is just what she needs to escape her disastrous love life.

The sun is shining and the locals seem friendly, even if the hotel staff do seem intent on playing matchmaker. But what better way to get over a broken heart than with a holiday fling? A sexy stranger who even makes a wetsuit look hot provides the answer, but is he all that he seems?

A series of mysterious disappearances leave Callie hunting for answers, and during her frantic search she finds it's not only the town that has secrets. Will she end up wishing she'd stayed at home with the ice cream?

For more details:
www.elise-noble.com/trouble-in-paradise

All the books in the Trouble Series are romantic suspense novels with a dash of added humour. Each story is a standalone—no cliffhangers!

If you enjoyed *A Very Happy Christmas*, please consider leaving a review.

For an author, every review is incredibly important. Not only do they make us feel warm and fuzzy inside, readers consider them when making their decision whether or not to buy a book. Even a line saying you enjoyed the book or what your favourite part was helps a lot.

Want to Stalk Me?

For updates on my new releases, giveaways, and other random stuff, you can sign up for my newsletter on my website: www.elise-noble.com

If you're on Facebook, you might also like to join Team Blackwood for exclusive giveaways, sneak previews, and book-related chat. Be the first to find out about new stories, and you might even see your name or one of your suggestions make it into print!

And if you'd like to read my books for FREE, you can also find details of how to join my advance review team.

Would you like to join Team Blackwood?

www.elise-noble.com/team-blackwood

facebook.com/EliseNobleAuthor

x.com/EliseANoble

instagram.com/elise_noble

goodreads.com/elisenoble

bookbub.com/authors/elise-noble

tiktok.com/@EliseNobleWrites

Also by Elise Noble

Blackwood Security

For the Love of Animals (Nate & Carmen - Prequel)

Black is My Heart (Diamond & Snow - Prequel)

Pitch Black

Into the Black

Forever Black

Gold Rush

Gray is My Heart

Neon (novella)

Out of the Blue

Ultraviolet

Glitter (novella)

Red Alert

White Hot

Sphere (novella)

The Scarlet Affair

Spirit (novella)

Quicksilver

The Girl with the Emerald Ring

Red After Dark

When the Shadows Fall

Phantom (novella)

Pretties in Pink

Chimera

The Devil and the Deep Blue Sea (2024)

Blue Moon (2024)

Blackwood Elements

Oxygen

Lithium

Carbon

Rhodium

Platinum

Lead

Copper

Bronze

Nickel

Hydrogen

Out of Their Elements (novella)

Blackwood UK

Joker in the Pack

Cherry on Top

Roses are Dead

Shallow Graves

Indigo Rain

Pass the Parcel (TBA)

Blackwood Casefiles

Stolen Hearts

Burning Love (TBA)

Baldwin's Shore

Dirty Little Secrets

Secrets, Lies, and Family Ties

Buried Secrets

A Secret to Die For

Blackwood Security vs. Baldwin's Shore

Secret Weapon

Secrets from the Past (2023)

Blackstone House

Hard Lines

Blurred Lines (novella)

Hard Tide

Hard Limits

Hard Luck (TBA)

Hard Code (TBA)

The Electi

Cursed

Spooked

Possessed

Demented

Judged

The Planes

A Vampire in Vegas

A Devil in the Dark (TBA)

The Trouble Series

Trouble in Paradise

Nothing but Trouble

24 Hours of Trouble

The Happy Ever After Series

A Very Happy Christmas (novella)

A Very Happy Valentine (novella) (2024)

Standalone

Life

Coco du Ciel

Twisted (short stories)

Books with clean versions available (no swearing and no on-the-page sex)

Pitch Black

Into the Black

Forever Black

Gold Rush

Gray is My Heart

Audiobooks

Black is My Heart (Diamond & Snow - Prequel)

Pitch Black

Into the Black

Forever Black

Gold Rush

Gray is My Heart

Neon (novella)

Dirty Little Secrets (2023)

www.ingramcontent.com/pod-product-compliance
Lightning Source LLC
Chambersburg PA
CBHW020634130626
46552CB00003B/1215